Timeline of Stone Age

This timeline shows some of the important events that took place during the Stone Age. Many useful things were invented during this period.

The first symbols are drawn at Blombos Cave, in South Africa. These abstract signs may have had special meanings.

Female clay figures called Venus figurines are made for thousands of years across central Europe.

Sickle and wheat

People start farming—keeping animals and growing plants in the Middle East and in China.

Start of the Iron Age

| 70,000 YEARS AGO | 35,000 YEARS AGO | 25,000 YEARS AGO | 20,000 YEARS AGO | 12,000 YEARS AGO | 2,000 BCE | 500–700 BCE |

Homo sapiens spread to North and South America.

Start of the Bronze Age. People start to make metal tools.

Modern humans in France and Spain live in caves, and make beautiful paintings in them.

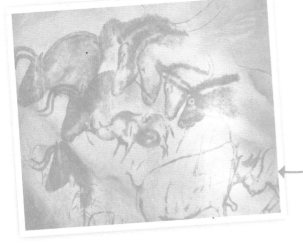

The Bronze Age began when metalworkers in the Middle East began using bronze. They made it by mixing two metals: copper and tin.

Bronze Age ax

This rock painting in Chauvet Cave, in France shows extinct animals such as woolly rhinoceroses, aurochs, and wild horses.

Things to find out:

DKfindout! Stone Age

Author: Klint Janulis
Consultant: James Dilley

Penguin Random House

Senior editor Marie Greenwood
Project art editor Joanne Clark
Editor Caryn Jenner
US Editor Rebecca Warren
US Senior editor Shannon Beatty
Design assistant Rhea Gaughan
Editorial assistant Kathleen Teece
Additional design Emma Hobson
Jacket design Amy Keast
Jacket co-ordinator Francesca Young
Managing editor Laura Gilbert
Managing art editor Diane Peyton Jones
Pre-production producer Dragana Puvacic
Producer Srijana Gurung
Art director Martin Wilson
Publisher Sarah Larter
Publishing director Sophie Mitchell
Educational consultant Jacqueline Harris

First American Edition, 2017
Published in the United States by DK Publishing
345 Hudson Street, New York, New York 10014

Copyright © 2017 Dorling Kindersley Limited
DK, a Division of Penguin Random House LLC
17 18 19 20 21 10 9 8 7 6 5 4 3 2 1
001–298649–Jan/2017

A catalog record for this book is available from the
Library of Congress.

ISBN 978-1-4654-5750-9

DK books are available at special discounts when
purchased in bulk for sales promotions, premiums,
fund-raising, or educational use. For details, contact: DK
Publishing Special Markets, 345 Hudson Street,
New York, New York 10014
SpecialSales@dk.com

Printed and bound in China

A WORLD OF IDEAS:
SEE ALL THERE IS TO KNOW

www.dk.com

BCE/CE
When you see the letters BCE, it means
Before the Common Era, which began in
the year 1 CE (Common Era).

Contents

Mammoth

Hand ax

Carved spear-thrower tip

Shaman

Neanderthal skull

Hunter with spear

Bone necklace

3

What is the Stone Age?

The Stone Age covers almost all of human history. It was the time when humans used stone tools. Through most of the Stone Age, people were hunter-gatherers. They looked for food by hunting, fishing, and collecting plants and fruit to eat. Gradually, early people developed to live in groups and communicate with each other, much like we do today. The Stone Age can be divided into three main periods, as shown here.

Old Stone Age (Paleolithic)

This is the biggest Stone Age time period as it covers more than 3 million years of human history. It is the time when people started to develop, or evolve, in many important ways, such as by making simple stone tools.

Flint hand ax

Harpoon tips

How people developed

Our ancestors learned to make stone tools and this allowed them to get food much more easily. Over many generations, this resulted in humans becoming cleverer and better at toolmaking, with larger brains and different bodies, eventually becoming the species we are today, *Homo sapiens*.

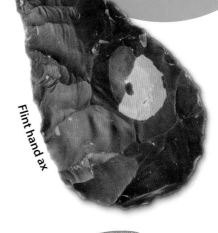

The shape and size of the skulls of early humans changed over time.

Early human
Living in Africa, Europe, and Asia between 600,000 and 200,000 years ago, *Homo heidelbergensis* is the direct ancestor of humans and Neanderthals. They could hunt, make complex stone tools, and use fire.

Old Stone age
3.3.million years ago–11,500 years ago

Middle Stone Age
11,500–6,500 years ago

New Stone Age
6,500–4,000 years ago

After the Stone Age
4,000 years ago

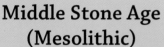

Neolithic polished ax head

New Stone Age (Neolithic)

"Neo" means "new," and it describes a time when people moved away from hunting and gathering, and became farmers in many parts of the world. However, people still continued to use stone tools.

Microliths (blade points)

Bronze Age ax

After the Stone Age

Some societies started to make metal tools during periods called the Bronze Age and Iron Age. However, to this day there are still people in the world living as hunter-gatherers.

Middle Stone Age (Mesolithic)

During this time, icy glaciers were melting and the seas were rising. People developed the tools they needed to deal with these changes. They became better at certain hunting skills, such as using harpoons (long spears) for catching fish.

Sickle for cutting grain

Iron Age helmet

Neanderthals had bigger eyes and brains than humans.

Homo sapiens had smaller brains than Neanderthals.

Neanderthal
Neanderthals (*Homo neanderthalensis*) are our closest relatives. They lived between 250,000 and about 24,000 years ago. They had bigger brains than humans and it is not understood exactly why they died out.

Homo sapien
Humans that looked like we do today appeared in Africa about 200,000 years ago, but we are not sure how similar their brains were to ours today. About 12,000 years ago, they had spread to most of the world.

Stone Age hunter

Stone Age hunters like this one lived toward the end of the Stone Age. They used animal skins to keep warm and to build shelters. They were skilled at making stone tools, rope and, fire. They were strong and capable, and true adventurers!

» **Species:** *Homo Sapiens*
....
» **Time period:** Late Stone Age
....
» **Where did they live:** Every continent apart from Antarctica

Meet a Stone Age human

Stone Age people had the same basic needs that people do today. We all need food, clothing, shelter, and companionship. But Stone Age people had to go out and hunt for their own food. They made their own clothes and shelters. In some ways, they were more skillful than we are today! Let's compare a Stone Age hunter with a modern adventurer …

Animal-skin shelter
When following herds of animals, people needed shelters that were quick and light to put up, like this one made from deer skin.

Stone Age human wears a tunic made from animal skin for protection from the cold.

Cordage
Cordage was rope made from plant or animal fibers. It was used for everything, including carrying firewood, making baskets, and building shelters.

Fire-making kit
Making fire was an essential skill. One way was to use a bow and a stick (drill) to create fire by friction. This was called the bow-drill method.

Stone tools
Stone tools helped people to cut down branches, hunt, and prepare food. Making stone tools was one of the first skills humans mastered, and was essential for their survival.

Bull roarer
This was a piece of wood or bone attached to rope that made a loud noise when spun around. It was a way of checking to see if other people were nearby.

Tent

Nylon tents used by campers today are lighter than Stone Age shelters. Instead of branches for the frame, they have thin aluminum poles that can be reused.

Today's human wears a waterproof jacket for protection from wind and rain

Rope

Campers use lightweight but strong nylon rope. It is similar to cordage, but even stronger.

Matches

Modern-day adventurers use matches, lighters, and fire starters to make fire out in the wilderness.

Knife

A multi-tool or Swiss Army knife can do many of the same things a stone tool can do, like cut, shave, pierce, or saw materials.

Mobile phone

Where would we be without our mobile phones? Today, people use their phones to communicate instantly with each other from afar.

Modern day adventurer

Modern humans do not need to hunt animals for food and skins to survive. They can go to a store to buy the food and equipment they need. The tools they use have been designed and made by specialists. Are they real adventurers?

» **Species:** *Homo Sapiens*

» **Time period:** Present day

» **Where do they live:** Every continent including Antarctica

Otzi the Iceman

The fully dressed body of Stone Age adventurer Otzi the Iceman was found in a glacier in the Austrian Alps. He was wearing a bearskin hat and had a waterproof cloak made of grass. Studies on his body showed that Otzi had been murdered by being struck with an arrow and then being hit on the head.

Stone Age arrowheads

! WOW!

Tattooing goes back to the Stone Age! Otzi had over **60 tattoos** on his body!

Where did they live?

Early in the Stone Age, the first people spread out from Africa to Europe and Asia. Eventually, over thousands of years, early people traveled across the world. They adapted to different environments, from the freezing Arctic to the hot, dry climate of Australia.

Settlers in Greenland hunted sea birds.

1 Greenland

People who settled in Greenland learned to hunt and find food in freezing ocean waters. They made boats and special tools for hunting in the ocean. Even today, some people still follow some of the same traditions.

GREENLAND
1

NORTH AMERICA

3
EUROPE

AFRI◄

SOUTH AMERICA
2

People in South America hunted llama and deer with stone tools.

2 Americas

North and South America are known as the Americas. These were the last areas to be settled. People spread across both continents, some living as hunter-gatherers, others as farmers.

People in Stone Age Europe hunted, fished, and gathered fruit and nuts.

3 Europe

People arrived in mainland Europe about 40,000 years ago. They reached the British Isles much later—near the end of the last Ice Age, around 10,000 years ago. These early Europeans had to cope with icy glaciers and very cold weather.

4 Africa

The first humans developed in Africa, where they began to walk on two legs and use stone tools. Some of these early humans evolved into modern humans, called *Homo sapiens*, our direct ancestors. These early people ate wild plants, and fished and hunted for food.

People in Africa learned to spear fish with sharp sticks in lakes and rivers.

5 Arctic

Humans need particular skills to live in the freezing Arctic. Many early humans that lived here became specialists in trapping animals and hunting, or they learned to manage herds of animals, such as reindeer.

Arctic people wore heavy furs to keep warm in the cold.

People made early clay pots in Japan.

The prehistoric megafauna (giant animals) of Australia are now extinct.

6 Japan

Humans arrived in Japan about 35,000 years ago. They were the first people to make their stone axes by grinding them instead of flintknapping (shaping flint).

7 Australia

Archaeologists don't know how early people traveled to Australia, but they quickly adapted to the hot climate. They would have faced animals such as giant turtles and marsupials as big as a cow!

Ice Age

When freezing temperatures cause ice to cover large parts of the world, this is called an Ice Age. There were several Ice Ages during the Stone Age, but the last major one started about 110,000 years ago. It lasted for many thousands of years, ending around 10,000 BCE. At its height, a third of the Earth was covered in ice. Living things had to learn to survive the cold. Ice Age humans made warm clothes and shelters from animal skins, fur, and bone.

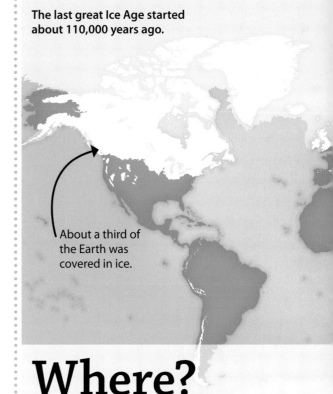

The last great Ice Age started about 110,000 years ago.

About a third of the Earth was covered in ice.

Where?

Ice sheets up to 2 miles (4 km) thick could be found on five of the Earth's seven continents during the last great Ice Age. Some of this ice still exists today in Antartica and Greenland.

Danger!

In many places, temperatures stayed below freezing throughout the year. People had to find ways of protecting themselves against the cold. Food became hard to come by because few plants could grow and many animals couldn't surive.

Humans

The first humans appeared and developed in Africa about 200,000 years ago. It was during a later Ice Age, about 130,000 to 90,000 years ago, that they started to spread. Over time, they traveled across the world.

Ice Age skull of a human

The ocean waters of the Arctic in the north and Antarctic in the south were also covered in ice.

Even today, Greenland is covered in ice.

Today's ice coverage

Shelter

People in the coldest parts of the world made huts. As trees couldn't grow in freezing conditions, they used animal bones to make the frames, and draped them with animal skins.

A Ukranian animal-bone hut

Animals

Some animals from the Ice Age have been found frozen in ice after many thousands of years. As well as mammoths, people have discovered woolly rhinos, horses, bison (buffalo), cave lions, and even puppies!

Woolly bison

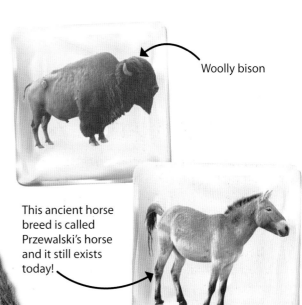

This ancient horse breed is called Przewalski's horse and it still exists today!

Clothes

Ice Age clothes were made out of animal skins, which were carefully cleaned and prepared first. Some clothes were decorated with thousands of beads. These clothes took years to make.

Ice Age shoes filled with dried grasses to help insulate from the cold.

11

Stone tools

People in the Stone Age regularly needed to cut meat, scrape skins, and cut up plants. Stone was the best and most common material around to make tools to do these tasks. The earliest tools were rocks that had been hit with great force to create sharp edges. As people began using stone tools for special tasks, different styles developed.

A straight blade was sharper than a hand ax.

Hand axes

Hand axes were one of the earliest and most popular tools in the Stone Age tool kit. They were especially useful for chopping meat, and were also used to break open bones and cut wood.

Blades

Blades were struck from larger pieces of stone. They had lots of different uses, including carving out pieces of antler and bone that could be made into other tools.

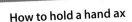

How to hold a hand ax

WOW!

People used to call **axes "thunderstones"** as they thought they were made by **lightning!**

Blade being used to carve an antler

Microliths

These are small, sharp points snapped off from blades. They could be attached to arrows, spears, darts, or harpoons (long spears used for fishing).

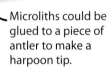

Microliths could be glued to a piece of antler to make a harpoon tip.

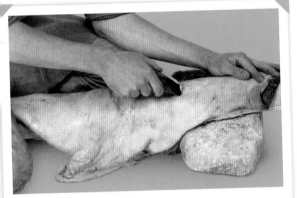

Scraper being used on an animal hide

The tip was used for scraping.

Scrapers

As their name suggests, scrapers were used to scrape flesh and hair from animal skins to make leather or furs. They had to be sharp enough to remove flesh, but not so sharp that they cut into the skin.

Axes

At the end of the Stone Age, people began farming. They needed more specialized axes so they could cut bigger trees to clear land. Some axes were made by carefully grinding very hard stone against rough rocks to create strong and sharp ax heads.

Ax being sharpened with a stone

On the hunt

Early people hunted almost anything that climbed, crawled, walked, swam, or flew. Animals were the main source of food necessary to survive in the Stone Age, especially in cold climates. This meant that people needed to invent effective weapons for hunting in order to stay alive.

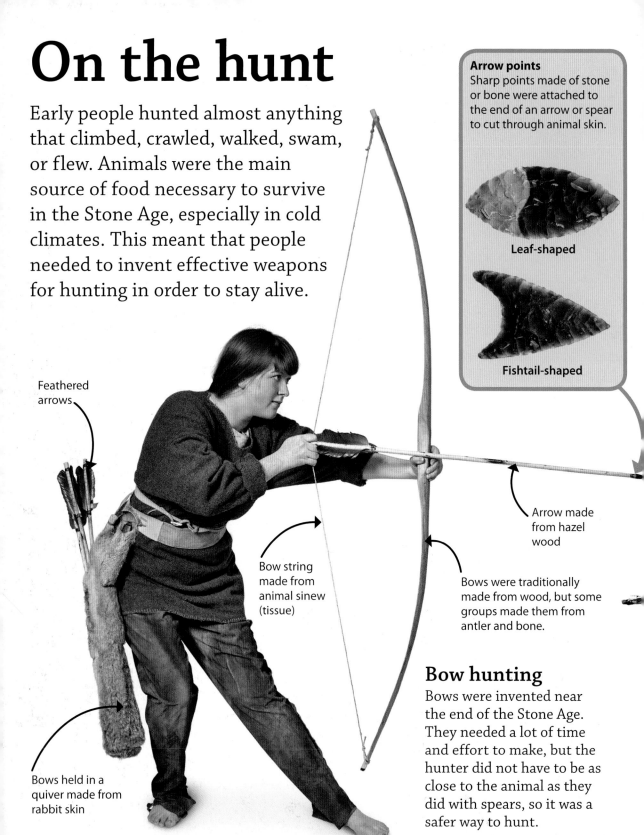

Arrow points
Sharp points made of stone or bone were attached to the end of an arrow or spear to cut through animal skin.

Leaf-shaped

Fishtail-shaped

Feathered arrows

Bow string made from animal sinew (tissue)

Arrow made from hazel wood

Bows were traditionally made from wood, but some groups made them from antler and bone.

Bows held in a quiver made from rabbit skin

Bow hunting

Bows were invented near the end of the Stone Age. They needed a lot of time and effort to make, but the hunter did not have to be as close to the animal as they did with spears, so it was a safer way to hunt.

Fishing

People fished in many ways. They waded into rivers and the sea to spear fish. They also used fish traps and hooks, and worked together using nets. This hunter is using a harpoon—a spear for catching fish.

Harpoon head
The pointed end of the harpoon was called the head, and it was often decorated with plant or bird shapes.

Spear thrower
This was a stick with a hook at one end to hold a spear. By throwing the spear using the thrower, the speed, distance, and power were increased.

Spear made from hazel wood

Spear throwing

The first spears were made for thrusting. They required the hunter to get close to an animal to wound it. This could be dangerous. Then people started making spears to throw. Some groups of people made spear throwers, so spears could be thrown even further.

What did they hunt?

Big animals, such as woolly rhinoceros, were dangerous to hunt. Some groups of people specialized in catching one type of animal, such as reindeer. Smaller animals, such as frogs and turtles, were easier to catch.

In the water
Early people caught fish and other animals in rivers and in the sea. Shellfish were collected on the coast. Fish could be dried, smoked, and stored, and provided a healthy diet.

Salmon

Seal

Trees and bushes
Birds nesting in trees and bushes, such as pigeons and ptarmigans, were hunted. Squirrels were also caught.

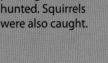

Ptarmigan

Land
People hunted all kinds of land animals, including hares, bison, red deer, wild boar, and horses.

Red deer

Hare

Stone Age animals

Many Stone Age animals would be terrifying to humans today! Herbivores (plant-eating animals) tended to be much larger than their modern relatives, which meant that many of the carnivores (meat-eating animals) hunting them were much larger as well. Large Stone Age animals are known as megafauna.

Tooth fossil

Saber-toothed cats

These large cats had long fangs that looked like a saber (sword) and could be up to 20 in (50 cm) long! Their sharp teeth could even pierce the hair and hide of larger animals. The most famous species was the saber-toothed tiger, found only in the Americas.

» Scale

Auroch skull fossil

Aurochs

The aurochs was a large ancestor of today's cows. Like modern cows, aurochs ate mostly grass. They survived much longer than most Stone Age megafauna. The last recorded example died in 1627. Aurochs are frequently seen on cave art.

» Scale

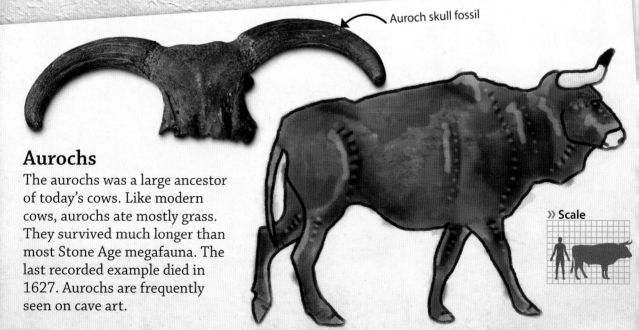

Woolly rhinoceros

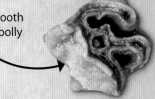

Related to modern rhinos, the woolly rhinoceros had a thick coat and a compact body suited for life in the cold grasslands of Northern Europe and Asia. Some of the woolly rhino's habitat is now underwater.

A molar tooth from a woolly rhino

Cave bears

Humans had to compete with cave bears for caves to live in. These huge bears ate mainly plants. Cave bears were related to American brown bears and weighed about 1,000 lb (450 kg) or more.

» Scale

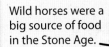

Cave bear tooth fossil

Still around today

Many of the animals that existed in the Stone Age are still with us today in a similar form to their ancestors.

Wild boar quickly adapt to new environments.

Wild horses were a big source of food in the Stone Age.

Many species of deer still exist across the world.

» Scale

Mammoths

Mammoths were one of the largest land animals living during the Stone Age and are one of the best known. Related to elephants, these giant animals were adapted to cold weather and were found in North America, Europe, Africa, and Asia. Much of what we know about them comes from mammoths that have been found frozen in ice.

Thick fur coat
The fur had two layers—a long outer layer and a thick, inner layer that helped protect, or insulate, from the cold.

Baby mammoth
Mammoth babies nursed from their mothers and stayed close by until they were old enough to defend themselves.

Lyuba

Lyuba was a baby mammoth found in the Russian Arctic in 2007 by reindeer herder Yuri Khudi. The mammoth was in such good condition that they knew what her last meal was! Lyuba was named after Yuri's wife to thank him.

The 41,800-year-old Lyuba is in Shemanovsky Museum, Russia.

! WOW!

Mammoths were still alive **4,000 years ago**—when the **Egyptian pyramids** were being built!

Tiny ears
The mammoth's ears were small to prevent them being damaged from the extreme cold.

Strong, sharp tusks
Mammoths may have used their massive tusks to fight each other with and as shovels to clear snow away from the plants they ate!

Hunted animal

The mammoth was a great source of food and tools for any Stone Age hunter lucky enough to hunt one or find a dead one. Their thick hair and body fat, large bones, and tusks meant the whole animal could be used—like having a Stone Age supermarket!

Mouth
Inside the mammoth's mouth were ridges that helped grind tough plants. They acted like a conveyor belt, moving the food to the back of the mouth as they chewed!

Feet
The soles of the feet had large cracks. This gave grip in the snow, like the tread on snow boots!

Mammoth sizes

There were a number of different species of mammoth. These pictures on the right show the sizes in comparison to an adult human.

Imperial mammoth
This huge mammoth was one of the biggest species, at about 16 ft (4.9 m) tall.

Woolly mammoth
This was about the size of an African elephant, at 11.4 ft (3.5 m) tall.

Pygmy mammoth
The pygmy was one of the smallest species, at 6.8 ft (2.1 m) tall.

Making tools

Early people used stone tools to chop up meat and cut plants and animal skins. The earliest stone tools, called choppers, were simple chunks of glassy rock that were sharp on one side. People made beautifully shaped tools called hand axes. Hand axes could be used for many jobs. They were the Stone Age person's "multi-tool."

Shaping rocks

Flint is a hard rock found in chalk and limestone. The shaping of flint and other stones to make tools is called flintknapping. Stone Age people learned to flintknapp from a young age. It was a skilled technique that took years to master.

The piece of rock being shaped is called the core.

Many of the flakes that come off the rock are still useful as cutting tools because they can be very sharp.

Leather clothing helped protect the flintknapper from being cut by sharp pieces of rock flying off at high speed.

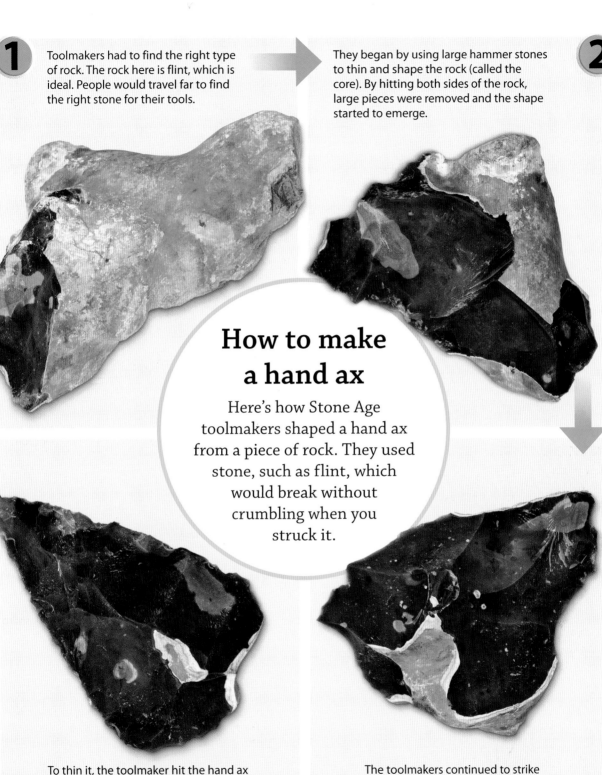

1 Toolmakers had to find the right type of rock. The rock here is flint, which is ideal. People would travel far to find the right stone for their tools.

2 They began by using large hammer stones to thin and shape the rock (called the core). By hitting both sides of the rock, large pieces were removed and the shape started to emerge.

How to make a hand ax

Here's how Stone Age toolmakers shaped a hand ax from a piece of rock. They used stone, such as flint, which would break without crumbling when you struck it.

4 To thin it, the toolmaker hit the hand ax with either a smaller hard hammer, such as a pebble, or by using a soft hammer, such as a piece of deer antler.

3 The toolmakers continued to strike each side of the rock. Each strike created a flat "platform" on which to create the next strike.

Forest foods

Before farming, Stone Age people relied on the forest for food and medicines. They were highly skilled at identifying the best plants and when and how to use them. If it was edible and tasted good, Stone Age people probably ate it!

Crab apples
Stone Age people gathered wild apples, such as crab apples. People of central Asia were they first to grow apples as crops.

Hawthorn
The berries stay on the trees late into winter and the tender leaves are eaten in the spring.

Plums
Full of natural sugar, many varieties of wild plum were gathered by Stone Age people.

Fruit
Wild fruit was the easiest source of sugar for early people. Children especially may well have enjoyed eating the sweet, ripe fruit. When people brought fruit back to camp, they would have scattered fruit seeds unintentionally, and so encouraged fruit to grow near their camps.

Sloe berries
These berries become very sweet after a frost. Otzi the Iceman had them in his stomach.

Blackberries
Blackberries grew wild and their brambles made good cordage (rope).

Elderflower
The berries need cooking before eating, and were usually made into drinks.

Poisonous plants

Stone Age people learned from experience to avoid poisonous plants. Some plants are not just poisonous to eat but may even be poisonous to touch. Remember to stay away from poisonous plants!

Holly berries
Colorful holly berries may be beautiful, but eating only a few will make both people and animals very sick.

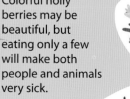

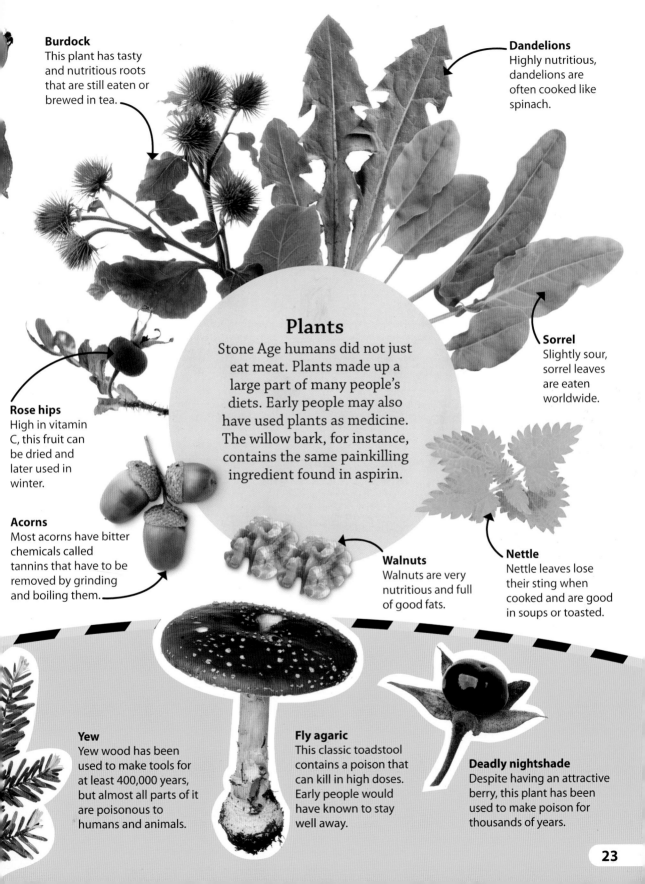

Burdock
This plant has tasty and nutritious roots that are still eaten or brewed in tea.

Dandelions
Highly nutritious, dandelions are often cooked like spinach.

Rose hips
High in vitamin C, this fruit can be dried and later used in winter.

Acorns
Most acorns have bitter chemicals called tannins that have to be removed by grinding and boiling them.

Plants
Stone Age humans did not just eat meat. Plants made up a large part of many people's diets. Early people may also have used plants as medicine. The willow bark, for instance, contains the same painkilling ingredient found in aspirin.

Sorrel
Slightly sour, sorrel leaves are eaten worldwide.

Walnuts
Walnuts are very nutritious and full of good fats.

Nettle
Nettle leaves lose their sting when cooked and are good in soups or toasted.

Yew
Yew wood has been used to make tools for at least 400,000 years, but almost all parts of it are poisonous to humans and animals.

Fly agaric
This classic toadstool contains a poison that can kill in high doses. Early people would have known to stay well away.

Deadly nightshade
Despite having an attractive berry, this plant has been used to make poison for thousands of years.

Shelter

Stone Age people needed good shelters to protect themselves from bad weather. Animal-skin huts were among the earliest types of shelter built. The frames were made from thin, flexible tree branches, and animal skins were draped over them. The materials were light enough to carry easily, making them ideal for the typical hunter-gatherer, who was always on the move.

Deer-skin hut

This hut is a recreation of a Stone Age shelter, and was made from about 40 roe-deer skins. Animal skin was ideal material for hut walls, as it trapped in the heat, so the insides were dry and warm. It was also easy to repair.

Flexible wooden poles often made from ash or hazel for the frame

Simple containers to carry food and tools

The top layers of skins overlapped the lower layers to keep water out.

Deer skin covered the floor for warmth.

Ax for cutting poles

Extra clothing and animal-skin blankets

What's inside

Take a peek inside this deer-skin tent to find out what you'd see in a typical Stone Age shelter. Woven baskets were handy for storage. Animal-skin blankets covered the floor, helping to keep the tent snug and warm.

! WOW!

Stone Age **roof-thatching techniques** are still used for houses in some parts of the world **today!**

Other shelters

While many people used animal skins to build their shelter, others used dried grasses. Caves were popular because they didn't have to be built!

Cave in Mongolia

Cave life
Caves offered immediate protection from wind, rain, and snow. But many were dark and damp and there was always the danger that animals, such as bears, lived there.

Humans and cave bears may have competed for the same cave.

Shelter made from grasses, England

Grass shelter
Simple grass shelters were used by some Stone Age groups during the winter. The careful layering of grasses is called thatching, and helps hold in heat.

Fire

Fire-making is a very ancient skill and one of the most important of the Stone Age. Once people started using fire, it provided many advantages. Fire helped people to keep warm, cook food, and to provide light for work in the evening.

Warmth

A warm fire is cozy and comforting to sit around, but for early humans this warmth would have been crucial for survival, especially in cold climates.

How people made fire

Early humans came across wild fires in forests, and then gradually learned how to make it themselves. One method of making fire using various handmade tools is called the bow drill.

The drill is a thick, pencil-shaped stick.

Step 1
A small nest from dried grass, called tinder, was made. Small pieces of dry wood, called kindling, were collected. These would be used to catch the first flame.

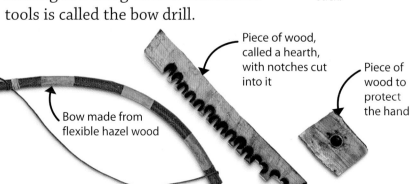

Bow made from flexible hazel wood

Piece of wood, called a hearth, with notches cut into it

Piece of wood to protect the hand

Nest of dried grass, called tinder

Small, dry sticks of wood, called kindling

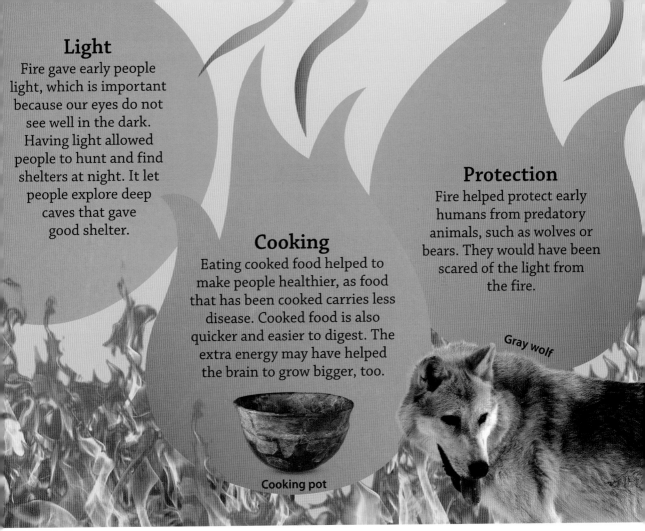

Light
Fire gave early people light, which is important because our eyes do not see well in the dark. Having light allowed people to hunt and find shelters at night. It let people explore deep caves that gave good shelter.

Cooking
Eating cooked food helped to make people healthier, as food that has been cooked carries less disease. Cooked food is also quicker and easier to digest. The extra energy may have helped the brain to grow bigger, too.

Cooking pot

Protection
Fire helped protect early humans from predatory animals, such as wolves or bears. They would have been scared of the light from the fire.

Gray wolf

Step 2
The tip of the drill was placed into one of the notches of the hearth. The bow string was wrapped around the drill. The drill was spun by moving the bow back and forth.

Piece of wood to protect the hand

Bow looped around drill

Step 3
As the fire-maker spun the drill faster, smoke appeared, and a red-hot ember formed. He then placed the burning ember by hand into the tinder bundle and blew on it.

Ember starts to smoke

Step 4
He continued to blow on the ember until it burst into a small flame. He set it on the ground and added the kindling, until it flared into a crackling fire.

Place the burning ember on the ground

A day in the life

During the Stone Age, it is believed that people lived together in close-knit groups of about three or four families. Children helped out with everyday jobs from an early age. This story imagines what life would have been like for a young girl called Tiya ...

The families had arrived at their summer camp. Tiya helped her grandmother put up the frame of their shelter. They used long flexible branches from the hazel tree and draped them with animal skins.

Some of the group were preparing to go hunting. Tiya wanted to join in, but she was too young just yet. She took a spear and started practicing.

That night, the hunters returned with their prize—a young bison. This would feed the group for weeks!

There were great celebrations around the campfire that night. The group sang songs and told stories. They played flutes made from bone and mammoth ivory.

Suddenly, Tiya heard rustling in the trees. She crept away to investigate and spied a wolverine! Though small, it was known to kill prey larger than itself.

Tiya knew she had to think quickly. She grabbed a spear, and hurled it. The animal stumbled and fell.

Tiya's grandmother led the group in congratulating Tiya for being brave and quick-thinking. She was now ready to join the next hunt.

Taming wolves

About 30,000 years ago, early people started to live and work alongside Stone Age wolves. These early wolves looked and behaved in similar ways to today's wolves. Over thousands of years, early wolves developed into the many breeds of dogs that we see today.

Wolves today
Stone Age wolves probably looked very similar to today's gray wolves, but they were even larger.

How it happened

Wolves were naturally drawn to early human settlements. They became used to searching for waste that people had left out, or even began to steal food.

Around the campfire
Some groups got used to having wolves nearby. They scared away predatory animals. Some wolves may have followed human camps.

Wolves and cubs
As wolves got used to being near people, they started to have their cubs nearby. Some people began feeding the friendlier cubs and wolves.

Wolf cubs tamed
Gradually, wolf cubs were adopted and tamed by people. These adopted wolves bred with each other, gradually creating a new species.

Living together
Stone Age people used these early tamed wolves to hunt with. The dogs also acted as guards and companions.

Stone Age clothes

Just as we do today, early people needed clothes to keep warm. In later Stone Age times, clothes were made from grasses and plant stems that were woven together to make fabric. Animal hides were also worn, and were especially useful in cold weather.

Leather outfit

This woman is wearing a tunic and trousers made from softened deer skin. Leather is very hardwearing, while giving protection from cold winds.

Necklace made from animal bones

Container made from tree bark

Legs stayed warm in leather trousers

There were no concrete sidewalks in Stone Age times, and people could quite easily walk on earth and grass in bare feet.

Summer worker

This woman is wearing a tunic made from the flax plant. At the end of the Stone Age, clothes woven from flax fiber were found to be ideal for keeping cool in warmer weather and for working.

Long sticks, called digging sticks, were used to dig up vegetables and roots. The stick was burnt at either end to make the points harder, so both ends could be used.

This spearhead is made from a rock called flint. Other spearheads were made from bone, antler, or ivory.

! WOW!

Some clothes were woven from the stems of **stinging nettles!**

Winter hunter

In the cold winter months, Stone Age people wore animal skins, such as this tunic made from red deer skin. Skins kept them warm while out hunting.

The dull brown color of the fur made great camouflage in woodland.

The belt has a pouch at the front for carrying stone tools.

This backpack is made from deer skin. The wooden frame is similar to metal frames found in modern rucksacks.

Spears were made from hazel or ash wood.

Shoes made from deer skin were sometimes worn to keep warm in the cold winter.

Needle and thread

Toward the end of the Stone Age, the needle and thread were invented to help make clothes. Once people could wear fitted clothing, it was easier for them to keep warm and to live in harsher climates.

Needles were made from bone and threaded with plant fiber.

How to survive the Stone Age

Klint Janulis, a former American Special Forces soldier, is now a survival instructor and Stone Age archaeologist at the University of Oxford, England. Klint studies how people survived in the Stone Age and how modern hunter-gatherer groups live to look for clues about how humans lived in the past.

FACT FILE

» **Name:** Klint Janulis

» **Born:** March 17, 1980

» **Favorite Stone Age tool:** Acheulean hand ax—"The Stone Age multi-tool"

» **Special skills:** survival, hunting, flintknapping, building shelters

Make a good shelter

"Surviving the Stone Age required technical skills, social skills, and intelligence. Knowing how to make a good shelter was essential. This could be made from leaves and grasses, animal skins, or if you were lucky, you might find a cozy cave."

Klint made this shelter from dried grass.

Hunting and trapping

"Stone Age people understood their environment—what plants they could eat, what types of wood were best for spears, where deer liked to bed down at night. Hunting and trapping animals, and fishing, were vital skills. For a Stone Age child, play was made up of learning the skills to hunt and trap."

Klint weaving a fish-catching basket

Fish-catching basket

Make fire

"Making fire was one of the most important Stone Age skills. It kept you warm, scared away dangerous animals, and cooked your food. Using fire in the Stone Age was as important as knowing how to use a computer today."

Make friends

"We make friends by helping each other out and sharing. Making friends in the Stone Age gave you advantages. If you wanted to hunt a large herd of animals, your friends and neighbors could help out."

Think ahead

"Early people learned how to plan for the future. This included storing extra food for later, when food was scarce. This is similar to people today saving money in the bank instead of spending it straightaway."

Grain could be stored

Beliefs

We can find out a lot about early people's beliefs by the burial sites they left behind. The dead were buried with tools and jewelry that would have taken months to make. Great ruins such as Stonehenge tell us that people were thinking about more than just hunting and gathering food.

Megalith

A megalith is a huge stone, or a collection of stones, that were used to mark a sacred place. The word comes from two Greek words meaning "big" and "rock."

Shamans may have worn animal skins to show their status.

Shamanism

Shamans were people who looked after the spiritual and physical well-being of the group. They held rituals to keep the community safe from evil spirits and used medicinal plants to treat illness.

Animal carving from Göbekli Tepe, Anatolia, Turkey

Göbekli Tepe

Göbekli Tepe is one of the most important Stone Age finds. It is a large series of stone buildings that have carvings of animals on them. It may have been a religious temple.

Most megaliths consist of several huge stones fitted together without cement.

Stonehenge

This circle of standing stones called Stonehenge is surrounded in mystery. Nobody knows exactly why Stonehenge was built or how it was used. It may have been a sacred monument, a burial site, a center for healing, or acted as a calendar.

Stonehenge, Wiltshire, England

Newgrange burial mound, County Meath, Ireland

Burial mound
At the end of the Stone Age, people were sometimes buried in burial mounds. These were large mounds of earth containing graves. They have been found all over the world.

Burial objects
The earliest objects to be buried with the dead were stone tools and red ochre (a mineral used to make paint). Jewelry and traces of wildflowers have also been found.

Bone necklace

Cow painted in red ochre

Horse painted in brown ochre

Cave painting

Thousands of years ago, the first artists painted colorful scenes inside caves. Among the most famous paintings are those found in Lascaux in southwest France. Many of the paintings show animals that people hunted for food. Stone Age artists looked closely at the animals and drew them very carefully and accurately.

! WOW!

Early people **blew paint** through **hollow bird wing bones**, making the first **spray paint!**

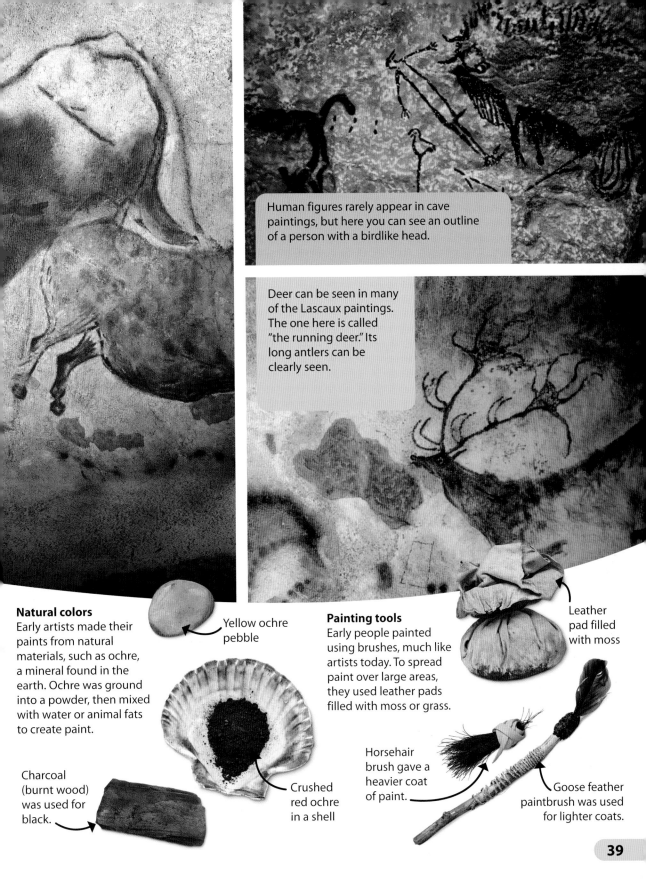

Human figures rarely appear in cave paintings, but here you can see an outline of a person with a birdlike head.

Deer can be seen in many of the Lascaux paintings. The one here is called "the running deer." Its long antlers can be clearly seen.

Natural colors
Early artists made their paints from natural materials, such as ochre, a mineral found in the earth. Ochre was ground into a powder, then mixed with water or animal fats to create paint.

Yellow ochre pebble

Charcoal (burnt wood) was used for black.

Crushed red ochre in a shell

Painting tools
Early people painted using brushes, much like artists today. To spread paint over large areas, they used leather pads filled with moss or grass.

Leather pad filled with moss

Horsehair brush gave a heavier coat of paint.

Goose feather paintbrush was used for lighter coats.

Caves of the world

Stone Age humans often made their homes in caves because they provided a ready made house and were often close to water, which would attract animals. People decorated these caves with magnificent prehistoric paintings, many showing animals. The artists may have painted to celebrate success at hunting or as a way of communicating with the spirit world.

Red buffalo
These cave paintings in Altamira Cave were the first ever found. They show animals including horses, goats, and buffalo. The paintings changed the way early people were viewed. Up until then, people did not think that early people could draw and paint.

Altamira Cave, Cantabria, Spain

Cave of Hands (Cueva de las Manos), Santa Cruz, Argentina

Cave of Hands
Early people in Argentina created these wonderful outlines of hands. They placed their hands on the wall and blew paint over the wall to create the painting. It may have been a way of leaving a signature or sign, perhaps for the spirit world.

Bhimbetka rock shelters, Madhya Pradesh, India

Hunters on horseback
Early people in India painted this scene showing men on horseback hunting with spears. These paintings are the earliest ever found in India.

The rock shelters shown from the outside

Warriors and dancers
Stone Age artists painted over a million pictures on rocks in the Kimberley region of Australia. Many show human figures hunting, running, or dancing, carrying bags, and wearing tassels and headdresses. These paintings are over 20,000 years old.

Bradshaw rock paintings, Kimberley, Australia

Stone Age detective

Archaeologists do more than dig up artifacts. To find out about life in the past, they use some of the same techniques as police detectives. For example, using chemicals to date artifacts tells us how old a material is or when it last saw sunlight. Archaeologists also make replicas (models) of Stone Age tools to find out how our ancestors might have used them.

The very dry landscape and geology in the Olduvai Gorge helped to preserve the Stone Age tools and fossils.

Olduvai Gorge

In the Olduvai Gorge in Tanzania, Africa, archaeologists have found traces of early humans that are more than 2 million years old. These include some of the earliest evidence of humans using tools to chop up animals, discovered from cut marks on animal bones.

Neolithic bowl

At the end of the Stone Age, pottery became more common to hold crops and food. By analyzing remains left in the pottery, such as dried food, archaeologists can work out what people ate. Similar pottery styles also help us to link cultures and communities.

Spiral meander design

Making stone tools required intelligence and skill. By studying how tools were made, archaeologists can determine the abilities of our early ancestors.

"The hobbit"

Often called "the hobbit" due to its small size, remains of this human relative were found on an island off the coast of Indonesia, where the water is very deep. Archaeologists are trying to work out how these people got to the island and why they were so small.

"The hobbit" skull

Markers show rock layers for studying (stratigraphy)

Digging deep

A basic rule of archaeology is that older stuff sits under newer stuff. Think of a messy bedroom with clothes piled on top of toys. The toys on the bottom of the pile have probably been there longer than the clothes on top! In this picture, the shells at the bottom have been there longer than the shells at the top.

Cheddar Man's skeleton

Cheddar Man

Cheddar Man is the name given to a body found in a cave in Cheddar Gorge, England, a place famous for its cheese. The caves in the gorge have a constant temperature, making them ideal for aging cheese as well as providing a comfortable home for Stone Age humans.

REALLY?

DNA evidence shows that **Cheddar Man** is a distant ancestor of some people living there today.

Meet the expert

Dr. Beccy Scott works at the British Museum in London, England. She is particularly interested in Neanderthals and is trying to find out how they survived in the area around the English Channel by studying their stone tools in detail.

Q: Could you explain what an archaeologist does?

A: Archaeologists use the traces (pieces) people leave behind to recreate what their lives were like. We might excavate (dig) the sites where they lived and recover objects that they left behind: stone tools, pottery, animal bones. We then study these things in detail—to see how they were made, and what they were used for.

Q: What inspired you to become an archaeologist?

A: I grew up near the chalk hills of Kent, England, so I was always collecting flints, trying to make arrowheads, and trying to find monuments marked on maps.

Q: What do you enjoy most about being an archaeologist?

A: I enjoy fieldwork the best. When you're digging, it brings you close to the people we're studying. You're recreating the actions of someone thousands of years ago. It can feel a bit spooky!

Q: What do you love about studying the Stone Age in particular?

A: I love that we only have evidence that Stone Age people left us to understand how they lived. It means you need a good imagination to open your mind to all possibilities!

Chalk cliffs on the coast of Kent, England, where Beccy grew up

Beccy enjoyed trying to make arrowheads as a child.

Q: What things have you learned about Stone Age people?

A: I mostly study the Neanderthals, and they never cease to surprise me. Archaeologists used to write about them as if they were hardly human. We now know that they were people just like us—they just had different ways of living.

Q: What is your most amazing find?

A: The find I'm proudest of is a henge! It was hard to see at first because the ditch was infilled with gravel. I was really pleased—not just that we'd found it, but that I'd stuck to my guns when no one believed me!

A henge is a Neolithic monument with a circular ditch and bank. This henge is in Derbyshire, England.

Q: Could you describe a typical day in your work?

A: If I'm in the field, then we get up early and spend the day on site digging. We remove sediment carefully with trowels, leaving all the stone tools exactly where we found them. Then we plot exactly where the tools are, and lift them one at a time. They go straight into bags with all the details of where they came from written on them. When we get back to our camp in the evening we make sure these details are put onto computers.

Q: What sort of equipment do you use?

A: It depends what I'm doing. We use shovels and mattocks, or pickaxes, then trowels, and finally, if you're cleaning around delicate bones or flints, we might use plastic tools. We hardly ever use brushes, despite what you see in films!

Q: What is the most difficult part of your job?

A: I'm not a very patient person, and sometimes you have to be patient as an archaeologist. It takes time to excavate carefully. You need to finish what you're doing, understand it, and then move on.

Q: Do you have any advice for future archaeologists?

A: Look at everything like an archaeologist! When you go to the beach, see how people choose to sit around, and the marks that they leave behind. How do the marks relate to what you saw? Imagine finding the contents of your pockets in the future: what would rot away, and what would people think about you based on what survived? You don't have to dig holes to be an archaeologist—it's a way of looking at people through things.

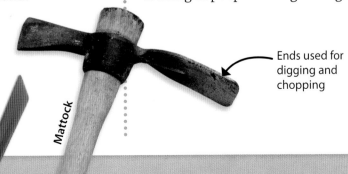

Plastic tool

Trowel

Mattock

Ends used for digging and chopping

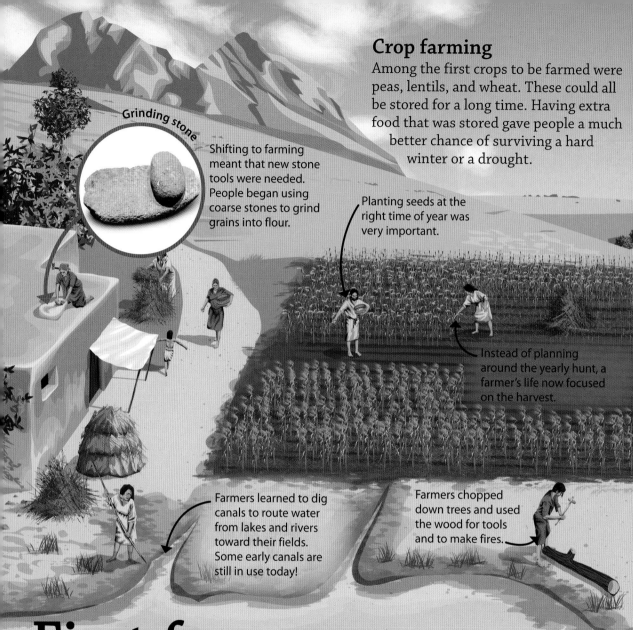

Crop farming

Among the first crops to be farmed were peas, lentils, and wheat. These could all be stored for a long time. Having extra food that was stored gave people a much better chance of surviving a hard winter or a drought.

Grinding stone

Shifting to farming meant that new stone tools were needed. People began using coarse stones to grind grains into flour.

Planting seeds at the right time of year was very important.

Instead of planning around the yearly hunt, a farmer's life now focused on the harvest.

Farmers learned to dig canals to route water from lakes and rivers toward their fields. Some early canals are still in use today!

Farmers chopped down trees and used the wood for tools and to make fires.

First farmers

Toward the end of the Stone Age, people started to farm in many parts of the world. Some settled down in fixed houses to plant crops and raise farm animals. Others kept small farms but continued to hunt and gather for most of their food. As farming developed and changed, so did the plants and animals that were being farmed.

Animal farming

Farming animals had advantages over hunting them. It provided a source of goods from the same animal year-round. To keep an animal such as a goat meant that you constantly had milk, and could cut its wool each year for clothing.

Some groups raised animals but were still nomadic, traveling from place to place.

Shepherds needed to keep a careful watch of their sheep to keep them safe.

Wild pigs were domesticated and kept in pens.

People used the flat roofs of houses as extra living space.

People cooked meat from the animals they raised on open fires.

Goats could be raised in dryer climates, as they needed little water.

REALLY?

All **large farm animals** share an important trait—they all **live in herds that have leaders.**

47

Stone Age village

A village in the Stone Age was quite different to a village today. People relied on each other for getting food and putting up shelters, and worked together as a group throughout the year. Not only did villagers know each other very well, but they lived closely together and would probably have been related.

Skara Brae

Skara Brae is a Neolithic (New Stone Age) site in the Orkney Islands. It was made almost entirely out of local rocks that are wide, flat, and stack very easily, making them ideal for building. The buildings give an amazing glimpse of Neolithic life!

The Orkney Islands are located off the coast of Scotland in the British Isles.

WHAT'S INSIDE

1 Fire hearth The fire was in the center of the house, allowing everyone to gather around. Dried seaweed or peat may have been burned.

2 Flat stones This site had very few trees to build with, but there were plenty of flat stones to build anything from walls to furniture.

3 Outside The houses were built into piles of waste with grass on top. This provided insulation against the cold climate.

4 Stone dressers Located in the same position in each house, these may have been used to show off goods or for religious purposes.

5 Stone boxes These were waterproofed with clay. People may have stored live limpets in the boxes to use as fishing bait.

6 Stone beds Animal hides and coverings would have made the beds more comfortable. Each house had one large bed and one small bed.

Village life

Many early Stone Age villages had shelters that could be moved easily so that people could follow animal herds for food and skins. Villagers may have come from different related families who lived apart some of the time and then came together for the hunting season. People would have needed to meet people from other villages and groups to find partners for mating!

A typical Stone Age village

WOW!

For more than **5,000 years, Skara Brae** was buried in the earth. In 1850, a **powerful storm** revealed the **Stone Age village**.

Arts and crafts

Weaving, sculpting, or basket-making are among the many arts and crafts that people enjoy today. But for early people, they were necessary tools for survival. The ability to make things gave people an advantage over those who could not. For instance, making a basket meant you could carry a lot more berries home.

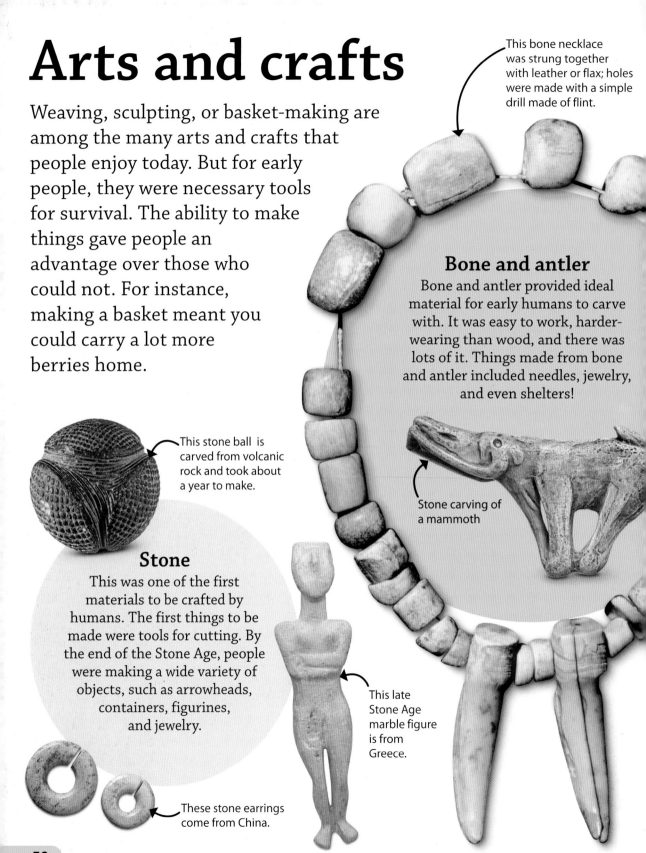

This bone necklace was strung together with leather or flax; holes were made with a simple drill made of flint.

Bone and antler
Bone and antler provided ideal material for early humans to carve with. It was easy to work, harder-wearing than wood, and there was lots of it. Things made from bone and antler included needles, jewelry, and even shelters!

Stone carving of a mammoth

This stone ball is carved from volcanic rock and took about a year to make.

Stone
This was one of the first materials to be crafted by humans. The first things to be made were tools for cutting. By the end of the Stone Age, people were making a wide variety of objects, such as arrowheads, containers, figurines, and jewelry.

This late Stone Age marble figure is from Greece.

These stone earrings come from China.

This clay animal may have been a child's toy.

Clay

Once Stone Age people started to settle they began to use clay to make containers. Clay pots were useful to cook food in and to hold dried food to protect it from animal scavengers. Groups that moved around a lot did not often keep pottery.

Heavy clay pots were used by settled communities.

Tree bark

People used bark from trees, such as birch and cedar, to make lightweight containers. These allowed people to carry food or water long distances and to store it for future use. Thicker wood from oak trees was useful for making ax handles.

Containers were made from bark or from woven grasses.

How people made rope

Rope-making (cordage) was one of the most important Stone Age crafts. It helped people to make containers, traps, and snares for catching animals. People could sew clothes, stitch together skins for shelters, and tie bundles together.

1

Find the right plant
The right plant needed to be found: one with long, thin, strong fibers, such as the nettle plant, shown here, was ideal.

2

Prepare the stems
The leaves were stripped from the stems of the nettle plant. While taking care not to get stung, each stem was then crushed with the thumb to soften it.

3

Strip the stems
The outer parts from the stems were carefully removed. The inner stem fibers were then left to dry out thoroughly.

4

Twist the stems
The fibers were twisted or braided so that they tightened against each other and became strong.

Bronze Age

The Bronze Age describes a period in time when some societies learned to produce tools made from bronze. At the same time, these societies become more dependent on farming and trade. The Bronze Age did not occur at the same time for all societies, but generally the Bronze Age followed the late Stone Age.

What is bronze?

Bronze is a mixture of two metals: copper and tin. When mixed together these two metals are both harder and more long-lasting than they are by themselves.

Hot, melting bronze being poured

Why was it so special?

Bronze is made from materials that were easy to mine. It is also an easy metal to melt and mold into shape. Bronze tools, such as axes and swords, were harder and more hard-wearing than stone tools.

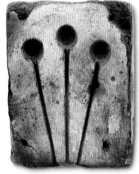

Mold for bronze pins

Finished pin in bronze

Weapons

Bronze Age societies were often at war with each other and this made bronze swords and armor important for their effectiveness when fighting.

Tools

Bronze tools, such as axes, were necessary to help clear land for farming. Flint tools were still being used by some Bronze Age people, but not to the extent they were in the Stone Age.

Late bronze ax head

Flint knife

Jewelry

Bronze Age jewelry was worn by the fashionable. Increases in farming and trade meant that some people became very wealthy. They used that wealth the same way some people do today, by owning jewelry.

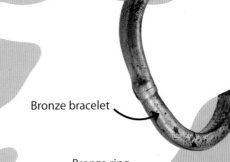

Bronze bracelet

Bronze ring

Sussex loops were bracelets that were bent double to form a loop.

When left out in the air, bronze oxidizes and turns green.

Bronze handle

Bronze sword

Trade

Farming and bronze toolmaking became big business in the Bronze Age. This encouraged the trading of new foods, clothes, and jewelry among societies across the world. It also created the need for an early form of coins—slabs of copper, or ingots, which had a standard value.

Copper ingot

Travel

Bronze Age societies began traveling further to buy and sell their goods. They built advanced ships and learned how to find their way (navigate) across great distances.

Rock carving from Sweden showing a boat

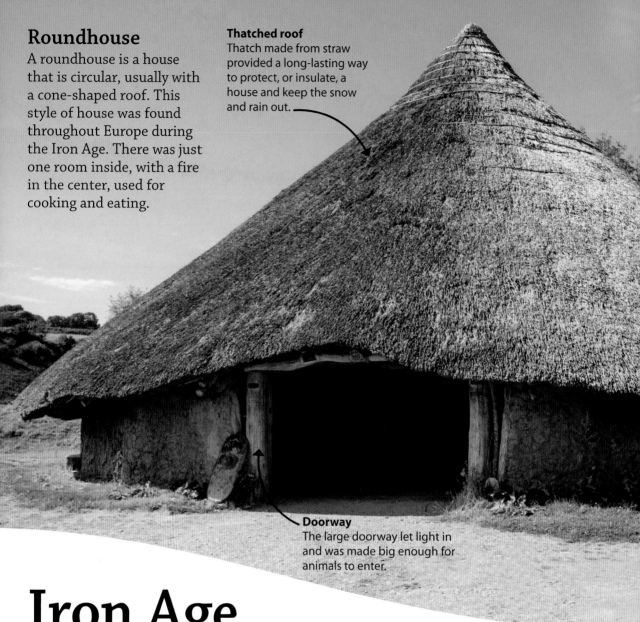

Roundhouse

A roundhouse is a house that is circular, usually with a cone-shaped roof. This style of house was found throughout Europe during the Iron Age. There was just one room inside, with a fire in the center, used for cooking and eating.

Thatched roof
Thatch made from straw provided a long-lasting way to protect, or insulate, a house and keep the snow and rain out.

Doorway
The large doorway let light in and was made big enough for animals to enter.

Iron Age

During the Iron Age, people started using tools and weapons made of iron instead of bronze. Iron is the most common metal on Earth. Iron tools have a sharper edge and are more durable than bronze. To make iron tools, raw iron from the Earth was heated in furnaces in a process called smelting. The advance in tools and weapons also led to changes in the way people lived.

Walls
The walls were usually made of stone or mud, to insulate against the cold. However, inside would have been dark and smoky.

Hill fort

A hill fort was an Iron Age village built on a hill, surrounded by walls made of earth and stone. The view from the hilltop meant that people could spot enemies approaching and defend the fort from attack. Many hill forts were also used to house animals.

Maiden Castle
This is a hill fort in Dorset, England, which was built during the middle of the Iron Age. About the size of 50 football fields, it was one of the largest hill forts in Europe.

Farming tools
Iron farm tools allowed farmers to clear the land much more efficiently than bronze. This meant farmers could produce more food with the same amount of work.

Model of plow

A plow pulled by a team of oxen was the Iron Age equivalent of a tractor.

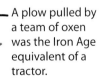

Weapons
Iron weapons were stronger and sharper than bronze ones, but required more care because they could rust.

Iron Age dagger in sheath

Today's hunter-gatherers

A hunter-gatherer is someone who gets their food from searching, or foraging, for wild plants and hunting wild animals. We all have ancestors that were hunter-gatherers. Today, there are just a few hunter-gatherer societies left. These people are highly skilled and take time to relax as well as work.

Hadza tribe

The Hadza people of East Africa are one of the last hunter-gatherer groups in the world. There are less than 1,000 Hadza people left and even fewer who still live as hunter-gatherers. These people have no written language, but have a fantastic history passed on by storytelling.

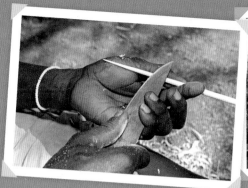

Hadza shelter
The Hadza move camps often, to adjust to the changing seasons and depending on what food is available. They can build a new shelter in an afternoon.

Poisonous arrow
This Hadza hunter is using a knife to shape and sharpen an arrow. He will then add plant poisons to the arrow tip.

Honey gatherers
The Hadza people have a special relationship with a bird called a "honey guide" bird. The bird leads the hunter to a beehive. On collecting the honey, they share this with the bird.

Camp fire
The Hadza pass the history of their people on by telling stories around the camp fire. These stories stretch back thousands of years.

Stone Age facts and figures

What we know about the Stone Age comes from the finds that archaeologists have dug up. Impress your friends with these amazing facts!

Ibex

Neanderthals had **large noses** to help them breathe in the cold air.

Obsidian is **SHARPEST** material on Earth!

Stone Age people used obsidian to produce very sharp blades. Today, it is still used for delicate surgery!

THE LAST MEAL

Otzi was a 5,000 year old man discovered in the Austrian Alps. His last meal was ibex (wild goat). Remains of it were found in his stomach, along with venison, grain, and berries.

10 A mammoth tusk could grow up to about 10 ft (3 m) in length.

Part of a fossilized mammoth tusk

11 There have been 11 Ice Ages over the last 4.6 billion years.

Adult hand

EATING **COOKED FOOD** GAVE PEOPLE EXTRA ENERGY FOR THEIR **BRAINS!**

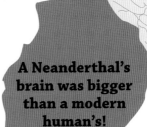

A Neanderthal's brain was bigger than a modern human's!

Birch-tar glue in a shell

GLUE was made by heating tree sap and mixing it with charcoal or ochre!

Homo sapiens means " **wise man** "

MEGALITH

MEANS "BIG ROCK"

100

The longest Ice Age lasted more than 100 million years!

40,800

The oldest cave painting is El Castillo in northern Spain. It is 40,800 years old!

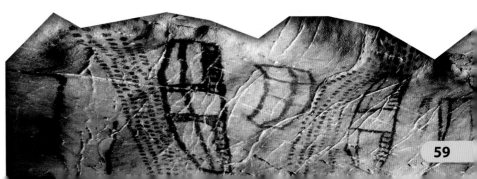

Glossary

Here are the meanings of some words that are useful for you to know when learning about the Stone Age.

antler Special kind of bone growth on the heads of male deer that can be used to make tools such as soft hammers or needles

beliefs Set of views that people hold about the world, life, and the afterlife

blade Type of stone tool that is long and has a very sharp edge

cordage Similar to rope, and usually made from plant or animal fibers, it can be used to make containers, shelters, and clothing

digging stick Long stick used to dig up roots and vegetables that grow under the soil

drill Narrow piece of wood spun on a hearth board (*see* hearth) to create enough heat to make fire

evolution Gradual process by which living things change over time to adapt to their environment

A flintknapper at work

foraging Gathering food that grows wild in nature

flax Plant that has natural fibers in it that can be made into cloth or cordage

flint Type of sedimentary rock that is very glassy, and produces a sharp edge when knapped

flintknapping *See* knapping

hammer stone Hard, rounded rock used to make stone tools such as hand axes out of glassy rocks like flint

hand ax Stone tools that could be used for cutting and chopping

harpoon Type of spear that is used when hunting from a boat on the water

hearth The place a fire burns in a shelter and the board used with a drill to make fire

horn Made out of the same stuff as your fingernails, horns grow on the head of some grass-eating animals. Also used to make containers and musical instruments

human Also called *Homo sapiens*, humans originated in Africa and have been around for at least 200,000 years

Microliths attached to a harpoon tip

hunter-gatherer People who get their food by gathering plants or hunting animals rather than through settled farming

Ice Age Period of time when the world is much colder, and many parts are covered in glaciers

kindling Dry, thin sticks of wood that can take the fire from the tinder and turn it into a bigger flame

knapping Process of creating stone tools by striking stone to remove material

megafauna Large animals such as elephants, woolly mammoth, and giant sloths. Many Stone Age megafauna are extinct today

megalithic Any structure made by using very large stones such as Stonehenge or Göbekli Tepe

meteorite Pieces from space that land on Earth. Some meteorites are made of solid metal and Stone Age people used them to make tools

microlith Small stone tools used to make the points for spears and arrows

Neanderthal These were our closest relatives and they died out 24,000 years ago

Neolithic Time period after the Mesolithic when humans began growing crops and raising animals

obsidian Type of volcanic rock that is extremely glassy and very sharp and was used to make cutting tools and ornaments

ochre Mineral that has a vivid color and is used for paint and dye when mixed with fat

Palaeolithic Longest time period of the Stone Age when humans learned how to make stone tools, fire, and hunt

scraper Simple stone tool used for scraping animal skins or wood to smooth them down

shaman Priest or spiritual leader who has special powers and uses these to guide their people on important matters

soft hammer Softer than a hard hammer, and often made of antler or wood, it allows a knapper to make a more precise and thin stone tool

spear thrower Tool for throwing a spear or dart a great distance with accuracy. The thrower acts as an extension of your arm giving you more power

thatching Technique for making a waterproof roof out of grasses and reeds.

tinder Thin material that easily catches fire

tusk Long tooth that grows from the jaws of animals such as warthogs, elephants, and mammoths. Sometimes called ivory, it can be carved easily and used to make jewelry and sculptures

Wolverine Ferocious animal that is in the weasel family and mainly scavenges meat. Wolverines appear frequently in Stone Age art

Index

Acknowledgments

The publisher would like to thank the following people for their assistance in the preparation of this book: Dr. Beccy Scott of The British Museum for the Meet the expert interview; Gary Ombler for photography; Andy Maxted of Royal Pavilion & Museums; Arran Lewis, Molly Lattin, and Dan Crisp for illustration; James Dilley (model & consultant) AncientCraft, Centre for the Archaeology of Human Origins, University of Southampton; Josie Mills and Tabitha Paterson for modeling; Cory Cuthbertson, Palaeolithic Researcher, Centre for the Archaeology of Human Origins, University of Southampton; Sally-Ann Spence of Oxford University Museum of Natural History; Neeraj Bhatia, Senior DTP Designer, and Nand Kishor Acharya, DTP Designer, for cut-out images; Garima Sharma and Surya Deogun for additional design.

My Findout facts:

Stone Age sites

KEY

- Cave painting
- Ancient shelter
- Village
- Burial site
- Human remains
- Religious site
- Stone tools
- Footprints

Kleine Feldhofer cave, Germany
Neanderthal bones discovered in 1856 were the first to show that Neanderthals were a different species.

Dent site, North America
Clovis points, a type of tool, were found here. They were thought to have been used to hunt mammoths.

Skara Brae, United Kingdom
Unearthed by a storm in 1850, this Neolithic village has stone houses that have been preserved.

Stonehenge, United Kingdom
This Neolithic religious monument consists of numerous layers of artifacts that were added to over time.

Cave of Altamira, Spain
These 18,500-year-old cave paintings have been preserved by a rock fall that closed the cave.

Cave of Hands, Argentina
Hand stencils and other cave-art styles, are evidence of early humans having lived in the Americas 13,000 years ago.

Lascaux cave, France
This cave features more than 2,000 figures painted in a unique style dating back more than 17,000 years.